**JAMES**

**PERCY**

Based on *The Railway Series* by the Rev. W. Awdry

Photographs by David Mitton, Kenny McArthur, and Terry Permane
for Britt Allcroft's production of *Thomas the Tank Engine and Friends*

First American Edition, 1991.
Copyright © by William Heinemann Ltd. 1990. Photographs copyright © Britt
Allcroft (Thomas) Ltd. 1985, 1986. All rights reserved under International and
Pan-American Copyright Conventions. Published in the United States by
Random House, Inc., New York. Originally published in Great Britain by Buzz
Books, an imprint of the Octopus Publishing Group, London. All publishing
rights: William Heinemann Ltd., London. All television and merchandising
rights licensed by William Heinemann Ltd. to Britt Allcroft (Thomas) Ltd.
exclusively, worldwide.

*Library of Congress Cataloging-in-Publication Data*
Percy runs away / [photographs by David Mitton, Kenny McArthur, and Terry
Permane for Britt Allcroft's production of Thomas the tank engine and friends]
1st American ed.    p.   cm.    "Based on the Railway series by the Rev. W.
Awdry"–T.p. verso. SUMMARY: Percy, a good friend of Thomas the Tank Engine's,
panics and runs away when he almost causes an accident in the train yard.
ISBN 0-679-82087-6   [1. Railroads–Trains–Fiction.]   I. Mitton, David,
ill.   II. McArthur, Kenny, ill.   III. Permane, Terry, ill.   IV. Awdry, W. Railway
series.   V. Thomas the tank engine and friends. PZ7. P4247   1991
[E]–dc20   91-8707

Manufactured in Great Britain   10 9 8 7 6 5 4 3 2 1

# PERCY RUNS AWAY

Random House

When Thomas the Tank Engine was given his own branch line, there was only Edward who would do the shunting for the big engines.

Edward liked shunting and playing with freight cars, but the others would not help him. They said that shunting was not a job

for important Tender Engines, it was a job for common Tank Engines.

Sir Topham Hatt was very cross. He kept them in the shed and said that they could only come out when they stopped being naughty. Then he sent for Thomas to come and help Edward run the line for a few days.

Henry, James, and Gordon were in the shed for several days. They were very miserable and longed to be let out.

At last, Sir Topham Hatt arrived.

"I hope that you are sorry," he said sternly, "and understand that every job on the railway is important." Then he told them that he had a surprise for them!

"We have a new Tank Engine called Percy. He is a smart little green engine, with four wheels. Percy has helped to pull the coaches, and Thomas and Edward have worked the main line very nicely, while you have been away."

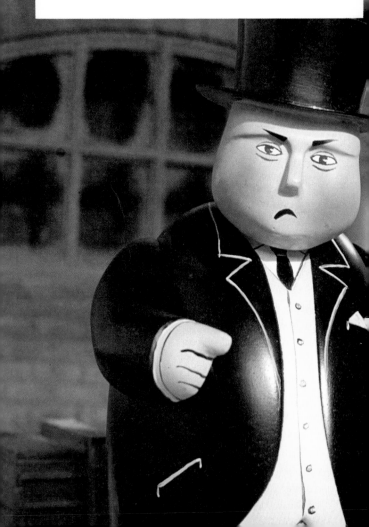

"But I will let you out now if you promise to work hard," he said.

"Yes, sir," said the three engines. "We will."

"That's right," said Sir Topham Hatt. "But please remember that this 'no shunting' nonsense must stop."

Sir Topham Hatt told Thomas, Edward, and Percy that they could go and play on the branch line for a few days. They ran off happily to find Annie and Clarabel at the junction.

Annie and Clarabel were Thomas's two coaches, and they were very pleased to see Thomas back again. Edward and Percy played with the freight cars.

"Stop! Stop! Stop!" screamed the cars
as they were pushed into their proper
sidings. But the two engines laughed and
went on shunting until the cars were in
their right places.

Next, Edward took some cars to the
quarry.

Percy was left alone, but he didn't mind a bit. He liked watching the trains and being cheeky to the other engines.

"Hurry, hurry, hurry," he would call, and they got very cross.

After a great deal of shunting on Thomas's branch line, Percy was waiting for the signalman to set the switch so that he could get back to the yard. He was eager to work, but he was being rather careless and was not paying attention.

Edward had told Percy about the signals on the main line.

"Be careful on that main line," he warned. "Whistle to the signalman to let him know that you are there."

But Percy forgot all about Edward's
warning.

He didn't remember to whistle, and
the busy signalman forgot he was there.

Percy waited and waited.

The switch was still against him, so he couldn't move. Then he looked along the main line.

"Peep! Peep!" he whistled in horror.

"Peep! peep!" he whistled again, for rushing straight toward him was Gordon with the Express.

Percy's driver turned on full steam and shouted for Percy to go back.

But Percy's wheels wouldn't turn quickly enough, and Gordon couldn't stop.

Percy waited for the crash. The driver and fireman jumped out.

"Oo...ooh!" groaned Gordon. "Get out of my way!"

Percy opened his eyes. Gordon had stopped with Percy's buffers just a few inches from his own. But Percy had begun to move backward.

"I won't stay here. I'll run away!" he puffed.

He went straight through Edward's station and was so frightened that he ran right up Gordon's hill without stopping.

After that he was tired, but he couldn't stop.

Percy had no driver to shut off steam and put on his brakes.

"I shall have to run till my wheels wear out!" panted Percy. "Oh dear! Oh dear! I want to stop! I want to stop!" he puffed.

The man in the signal box saw that Percy was in trouble, so he kindly set the switch.

Percy puffed wearily into a nice empty siding.

He was too tired now to care where he went.

"I–want–to–stop! I–want–to–stop!" he puffed.

"I have stopped! I have stopped!" he said, thankfully.

"Sssh...Sssh!" he gasped as he ended up in a big bank of earth.

"Never mind, Percy," said the workmen as they dug him out. "You shall have a drink and some coal, and then you'll feel better."

Gordon had arrived.

"Well done, Percy! You started so quickly that you stopped a nasty accident!"

"I'm sorry I was cheeky," said Percy.
"You were clever to stop."

Then Gordon helped to pull Percy out
from the bank.

Now Percy helps with the coaches in the
yard. He is still cheeky because he is that
sort of engine, but he is always *very* careful
when he goes on the main line.

**THOMAS**

**EDWARD**

**GORDON**